.. **E**

Petra Lloyd

First published in Wales 01/01/2014
Copyright © Petra Lloyd

All rights reserved. No part of this publication may be reproduced, stored in a retrieval system or transmitted in any form or by any means without the prior permission in writing of the publisher, nor be circulated in writing of any publisher, nor be otherwise circulated in any form of binding or cover other than that in which it is published without a similar condition including this condition, being imposed on the subsequent purchaser.

This book has been produced for the Amazon Kindle and is distributed by Amazon Direct Publishing

This is a work of fiction. Names, characters, places and events are the product of the author's imagination. Any resemblance to persons or places is purely coincidental.

Introduction

Ben had always wanted a dog of his own. When his stepfather said that he was allowed one Ben couldn't believe his luck. Was everything quite as it seemed for Ben and his dog, Blue, or was there something far more sinister taking place behind the scenes?

Chapter One

"Here, lad. Take it!" Ben's father handed him a five pound note.

"Gosh, thanks Dad," said Ben. His stepfather wasn't usually a generous man and Ben rarely had pocket money. He handed a couple of twenty pound notes to Ben's mother too.

"Go and treat yourself to a new pair of shoes or something, Lucy." William said. She took the money and put it into her pocket and looked down at her worn leather shoes. She did need a new pair but she knew also that there wouldn't be much left for anything after the weekend shop.

"Did you get lucky with a scratch card?" she asked.

"Something like that," William said. "I won a bit on the dogs last night." Lucy tried to hide the frown that spread across her face. She wished that her husband wouldn't waste so much money and time at the betting shop. He seemed to be there at least twice a week, sometimes for several hours an evening and rarely brought any money home. He took himself off to the job centre regularly but, although he was offered a few jobs, he never managed to keep them for more than a week or two.

He wasn't at all like Ben's father, George. He had been a real worker. He and Lucy had run a small shop and post office together. When times got hard they had to close the shop and sell up. It had hit them badly, having to give up the home that they had worked so hard for, and she was distraught when he was taken ill and later died of heart failure. Long hours and worry, the doctor said. Ben had been two years old when he lost his dad and could not remember much about life in the old home. William had been there for her after George died and got on well enough with Ben but he had changed over the years. He used to be a kinder man; never one to show his feelings much, but he had provided support and a home for them all and she was grateful for it. At times she felt that she could have done better for Ben but the lad seemed content enough and did call William "Dad".

"Could we have a dog?" His mother gave him a sideways look.

"Dogs cost money, Ben, and things are a bit tight until William finds regular work."

"Not much chance of that!" William grunted. "I'd thought about getting a dog though." Ben looked surprised. He'd wanted a pet for years but he'd had never allowed him to have one, not even a hamster when a friend had some to give away when they were in primary school. He'd never thought that his stepdad was an animal person. He didn't think that he even liked dogs much apart from the ones that ran around race tracks. He always seemed to find money to place bets on them.

"We'll see if we can find one this weekend," said William. "It'll have to be one that is being given away though. I can't afford to get one of those nonsense designer dogs! The free ads paper comes out today. We'll have a look in there." Ben didn't know what had made his stepdad change his mind but he didn't really care. He made his way to school, wanting the day to be over as quickly as possible so that they could look for a dog.

"Keep your mind on your work, Ben!" said his English teacher. "You're miles away today."

"Sorry, Miss!" Ben mumbled. He wasn't really interested in Dickens and his descriptions of poverty in Victorian London that day.

"Perhaps you could read the next page aloud?" asked Miss Lowe. Ben stared at his book. He hadn't been listening and he didn't know what page he was supposed to read.

"Page seventeen, Ben!" Miss Lowe was starting to sound irritated. Ben read the page and the next one too before he was asked to stop.

"Thank you, Ben," said Miss Lowe. "Come to have a word with me afterwards." For the rest of the lesson Ben worried that he'd get detention and would have to stay behind after school. He'd miss the bus and would have to walk the three miles home if that happened.

At the end of the English lesson he waited at Miss Lowe's desk. She reminded the class to get their homework finished and handed in by the following Monday and then turned to Ben.

"Your mind wasn't on your work at all today, Ben.

Is anything worrying you?" she asked. Ben looked sheepish.

"I'm sorry, Miss. There's nothing wrong. It's just that..." he hesitated for a moment thinking that it would sound silly but in the end he told her that his dad was going to get him a dog.

"Well, if that's all it is you must keep your mind on your work in future. Now go and get some fresh air. You're missing break." Ben was relieved not to have had a row. Miss Lowe was ok really, he thought. The rest of the day dragged even more than usual. Eventually the school bell rang and it was home time. He threw some books into his bag and hurried to get his coat. He always looked forward to the weekends but this one might turn out to be better than most.

When he got home he found William sitting at the kitchen table with a can of cola in his hand, browsing through the small ads in the paper.

"Hi Dad!" he said.

"I might have found a dog, Ben," William said. Ben looked at the advert that his stepfather was pointing to.

Staffordshire bull terrier bitch.
Five years old.
Black in colour. Lovely nature.
Owner cannot keep any longer due
to a change in circumstances
Free to good home

A staffie, he thought. They're really cool!

"Give them a ring, Dad!" William picked up the telephone and dialled the number. After a few rings a woman answered.

"I've just read your ad about the staffie," he said. "Have you found a home for her yet?" Ben was a bit amused at his telephone voice. He was trying to sound posh. Ben crossed his fingers and willed her to say that she hadn't. They talked for a few minutes and William scribbled down an address on a scrap of paper.

"She lives a few miles away. I said that we'd drive over this evening to see the dog," said William. "We'll wait until your mother gets back from work and we'll drive over there after we've eaten."

Chapter two

William and Ben set off in the van to find the address where the woman lived. It turned out to be a terraced house at the end of a small row. They parked the van outside, and made their way to the door. Ben rang the doorbell. They heard footsteps and then the door was opened by a woman with a lovely smile and clothes that could best be described as comfortable.

"I'm Alice Finch," she said. "Do come on in and meet my little lass." She led the way along a narrow corridor and into a small sitting room.

"Sit yourselves down and I'll let Daisy in to say hello. Can I make you both a cup of tea?" she asked. They refused the offer of the tea as Ben was eager to meet her dog. The door was pushed open and a nose appeared followed by a very lively dog with a friendly tail, and a really glossy dark coat. She went straight up to Ben. He put out his hand to give her a pat and she held up her paw.

"Hello Daisy!" said Ben.

"She likes to shake hands when she meets new friends," explained Mrs. Finch. "I can tell that she likes you."

"She's lovely!" said Ben as he smoothed her coat with his hands. "Can we take have her? We'll take really good care of her."

Mrs. Finch told them that she had owned Daisy ever since she was a six week old pup. She couldn't keep her anymore because her heating bills and rent had risen so much lately that she could no longer afford to live alone. She had to move away to live with her daughter. She had a cat and wouldn't have Daisy in her house. She wanted to find a good home for her where she would be loved and well cared for.

"She's been a wonderful friend to me," she told them. "I will be very sad to see her go but I can see that you will be kind to her. I have had several phone calls from lads wanting her but I want her to go to a family where she'll be loved and looked after."

"Has she ever had a litter of pups?" asked William.

"Pups? No, she's never had pups. She's not been neutered though. I couldn't afford to take her to the vet but I don't let her out on her own anyway. She's such a friendly lass that anyone could have pinched her if they'd had a fancy to. You hear about dogs going missing all the time and I would have hated to lose my Daisy."

"I'll take her out for walks before school every day," Ben told her.

"We will take proper care of her," William assured her. Mrs. Finch looked really sad at the thought of saying goodbye to her companion but was sure that it was the best thing for Daisy. She couldn't keep her now and couldn't bear the idea of putting her into the local dogs' home where she would be put to sleep if a suitable home couldn't found for her.

"What d'you think Ben? Shall we take her?"

"Yes, can we?" asked Ben, grinning.

"I'll get her things," she told them as she made her way to the hall. Moments later she came back holding a large carrier bag.

"I've put her favourite blanket in here and her food and water bowls too, and her toy. She likes to take that with her when she goes to her bed for the night." Mrs. Finch handed the dog lead to Ben and he reached down and clipped it to Daisy's collar.

She had tears in her eyes as she patted Daisy for the last time and told her to be a good girl for her new owners. She watched sadly as Ben and his stepfather led Daisy out of her home and to the van. The dog jumped inside, quite happily, and William closed the back door.

Ben was excited as they drove home and chatted about how he would take Daisy out on weekends and maybe early morning walks too.

"I don't really want to call her Daisy though, Dad. My friends would laugh if they heard me calling my dog that."

"Think of something else, then!" said William.

"She's got a lovely coat, sort of blue black," said Ben. "Can I call her Blue?"

"Aye, that's as good a name as any," grunted William.

When they arrived home Ben took the dog along the path towards the house.

"Hang on, lad!" William shouted. "We'll put her in the old shed for the night. She'll be ok there." Ben was taken aback. The dog needed to live inside with him, not in a cold, dark shed. He knew better than to argue with his stepfather though. William was a bit too quick to react angrily when he got cross with Ben so he wasn't going to risk any disagreement that evening. Reluctantly he led Blue to the shed. He put the blanket that Mrs. Finch had sent into one corner and fetched some water to fill the bowl from the outside tap too. He stayed with her for a few minutes before William called to him to come in to the house.

"I don't want you making a big fuss of that dog," he said. "She's got to earn her keep!"

Ben was very upset as he left Blue in the shed. As he walked along the path to the house he could hear her howling softly. Maybe she'd be allowed to come to live in the house tomorrow, he thought. Perhaps they want to buy her a proper dog basket or something before she'll be allowed inside. And how was Blue supposed to earn her keep if she was out in the shed? She couldn't be any sort of a guard dog there.

Ben could hear Blue howling as he lay in bed that night. He was really upset that she had to spend her first night out in the shed. It would be cold for her and she wasn't used to being on her own.

Chapter Three

Early the next morning Ben got up and dressed quickly. He had decided to take Blue for a long walk so that they could get to know each other. His folks weren't up and about yet. They often had a lie in on a Saturday. Ben opened the shed door to find Blue lying on her rug where he had left her.

"Hello Blue! Come here, lass!" Blue looked up at Ben and then ran towards him, wagging her tail and pleased to have some company. He patted her coat and then bent down to give her a hug. She licked his face and wagged her tail even more. Ben took her out into the small garden where she had a good sniff and then to the kitchen to see what he could give her to eat. Mrs. Finch had packed two tins of dog food and a small box of biscuits. He opened one of the tins and emptied the contents into a cereal bowl and put it down on the floor. Blue wolfed it down really quickly. She'd been hungry and a bit cold too after her night in the shed. He looked around for her lead.

"Is that you down there, Ben?" He heard his mother's voice calling from upstairs.

"Put the kettle on and I'll be down to make some tea." Ben filled the kettle and put it to boil. His mother came down, wearing her dressing gown and slippers.

"So this is the little dog!" she said, putting her hand

out for Blue to sniff.

"She's a super one! I don't know what made your stepdad change his mind about getting you a pet though."

"I don't either but I'm so pleased that he did. I love Blue already!" He patted the dog and stroked her soft fur. "Dad made her sleep out in the shed last night. She was crying too. I heard her when I was trying to sleep."

"Well, she's a member of our family now so she can live inside," said Lucy. "We can't have a super little lass like you out in the cold, can we?"

Blue seemed to like being there with her new owners and was getting to know her new name. Lucy made some tea and handed a mug to Ben. Blue settled on the floor of the kitchen, keeping one eye open so as not to miss anything.

"I'm going to take her for a walk, Mum," said Ben.

"Well, don't be too long. I'll have some breakfast ready when you get back." Ben and Blue set off round the village. She walked nicely on her lead, not pulling at all, and Ben couldn't have been more delighted to have a dog of his own. He took her to the park but decided not to let her off her lead just in case she ran off. They walked back along the path by the canal and Ben took the shortcut home and soon they were at the back gate. Ben opened it and led Blue into the garden. She pulled back a little as they walked towards the garden shed.

"It's ok, girl!" he reassured her. "You're coming to live in our house from now on. You don't ever have to go back into that shed."

Chapter Four

William always went to the pub on a Saturday afternoon. He enjoyed a pint or two and that day was no exception. The Crown was a rough place where men went to drink and not much else. The walls were probably cream once but over the years had become nicotine stained and the paintwork was peeling and none too clean. He ordered a pint and went to sit by the fire, the only redeeming feature of the otherwise dingy place.

"Hi Will. How's it going?"

"Tom! It's going well, mate! I've a bit of news for you," said William to his friend. "You know that I wanted a dog of my own?" Tom nodded. "Well, the lad and I went out last evening and got ourselves a fine staffie bitch. She's a bonny one too!"

"She been in the ring?" asked Tom

"No way, at least not yet! She was an old lady's pet but I reckon I could get some fight out of her with a bit of work."

"A youngster then, Will?" William shook his head.

"No, she's a five year old. I still think that I could do something with her though."

Tom frowned. "You won't get a dog of that age to

do much. She's past it if she's been a pet. Best you could do is to use her as a bait dog."

"Aye, maybe!" said William. "Be a bit of a waste though seeing as I've only just got her and she looks a good sort."

"Get some puppies from her then and breed yourself a strong dog. You could train him up from a pup."

William nodded. "Hmm, maybe!"

"Jack's got a couple of fine dogs up at the farm. He's kept 'em out of the ring and just uses 'em for breeding. They're good stud dogs; strong with good jaws."

"Sounds a plan," William said as he finished his pint.

"Want another?" Tom asked, pointing to William's empty glass. The two men stayed by the fire talking and supping pint after pint until the early evening.

"Better be getting back!" said William. "Lucy will have food on the table for me by now. She always does toad in the hole on a Saturday and I told her that I wouldn't be too late in."

"She's a decent lass, your Lucy!" Tom said. "How do you get away with spending so much time up at Firs Farm then?"

"I don't really lie to her," William grinned. "I tell her that I'm at the dogs and she thinks I'm round the betting shop watching the greyhounds! I won a couple of hundred at the farm last time and I slipped her some to treat herself to something. She's happy!"

Tom laughed. "Let's hope that she never finds out where you've really been then. I can't imagine she'd be too happy if she knew that you were in with the Firs Farm Lads."

"She'd not be happy at all if she knew the half of it," said William as he got up to make his way home, leaving Tom to down a few more pints.

As he walked back he thought more about putting Blue in pup. If she produced a decent litter from a champion dog they'd be worth a packet. There were always buyers to be found for good young dogs and the sons of champions were worth more than their weight in gold.

When William arrived home he was greeted by some wonderful cooking smells.

"That's not toad in the hole!" he said as he bent to kiss Lucy. She pushed him away.

"You stink of ale, William. Go and have a wash and brush up before supper," she said, a little crossly. She had to work long hours at her cleaning job to bring money into the home and she disliked William wasting cash on beer. They sat down to supper of roast pork and all the trimmings.

"You've made a grand supper this evening," he said. "How come?"

"Well, we don't usually have a decent roast so I got this as a bit of a treat. The lad needs to eat better than our usual Saturday supper."

"I love toad in the hole, Mum," said Ben, "but this is way nicer. If there's any left can I give some to Blue?" Lucy smiled at Ben but knew that she couldn't really afford to use good meat on the dog. Any leftovers would be sliced up for sandwiches.

Blue sat quietly beside Ben, watching every mouthful that he ate, but not begging or making any kind of a fuss.

"Mrs. Finch trained her well," he said.

"Aye, she did!" William thought that they'd managed to gct a good dog in Blue. If she bred some strong dog pups he had a mind to train one or two up for the ring.

Chapter Five

A day or so later William drove up to Firs Farm to speak to Jack about putting Blue in pup.

"It'll cost you a bit," Jack told him. "Which dog have you got in mind?"

"I've a fancy to use your Bruno," he said.

"Have you now?" asked Jack, raising an eyebrow. "I'm careful with him. He throws good pups and he's not going to be cheap. He's a grand champion is Bruno."

William had seen Jack's best dog in the ring at least three times and he was a great beast of an animal; strong as an ox and with spirit to die for. In fact that was what had happened to most of the dogs that Bruno had been matched against. He could train up a fine dog from one of his pups, he thought. If it turned out to be a half as good a fighter as Bruno he'd make a lot of money out of him. Even a half decent dog could be a good earner if he had only one or two fights out of it. The more he thought about it the more he liked the idea.

"So, how much?" William asked.

"One thousand pounds for the stud fee and if your bitch doesn't take the first time I'll let you bring her back for free," said Jack, holding out his hand for

William to take to seal the deal."

"Come off it, Jack! That's far more than I can afford." William knew that champion dogs cost good money but that was high, even if he would make a few thousand out of a decent fighting dog eventually. "I don't have that sort of cash and you know it."

"Put her to one of the other dogs then! You'd get good pups with them as sires." William shook his head.

"No, it's your Bruno that I've got my eye on."

"Ok," said Jack, "I'll do a deal. You let me have the pick of the litter, a male dog mind, and you can bring your bitch here for five hundred pounds and put her with Bruno. That's a good offer." William knew that he wasn't going to get a better price and the two men shook on that.

"Just bring her here as soon as she's ready and we'll see what Bruno can do." Jack was putting his some of his younger dogs in the ring later and invited William to stay.

"The boys from the city are coming over and we'll have some hot bets on," Jack told him. "We'll have some of the best dogmen here." William was tempted but had promised to be home earlier that evening. Lucy knew what time the betting shop closed and he didn't want push his luck and arouse suspicion. She'd probably think that he had wasted his time and money at The Crown if he was too late.

He would need to keep a careful eye on Blue to see

when she was ready to go to Bruno. It was rather too good an opportunity to miss, William thought.

It was about ten days later that Blue came into season and was ready to be served. William had managed to get the stud fee together one way or another although he had left Lucy very short of housekeeping money. He'd sold a gold brooch that belonged to her too; a birthday present from her first husband. She kept it rolled inside a piece of tissue at the bottom of her jewellery box and hardly ever wore it. He knew that it would be months before she noticed that it had gone. He had taken it to the gold buyer in the market and had a good price for it and, with that, he was able to scrape the five hundred pounds together.

Still, in a few weeks' time he'd have a dog to train up and then it should earn him some really big money eventually. He'd seen well over five thousand pounds change hands at a single match in bets and, if he could produce a great dog with the same killing instincts as Bruno, all the champions in the county would be coming to his door wanting to take it on.

William took his phone out of his jacket pocket and dialled the telephone number of Firs Farm. After two rings it played the answerphone message.

"Jack? Pick up if you're there!"

"Will! What's up, mate?"

"I've got the bitch ready for your Bruno. Can I bring her round?" asked William.

"Yes, ok, but bring her round in the next half hour if you can," said Jack. "I've got stuff to do." It was a school day and Lucy was at work so William reckoned that he'd be there and back with Blue and she and Ben would be none the wiser. He called her to him, slipped on her lead, and led her outside. He drove her off to Jack's place was there within twenty minutes. He went out to look for Jack, leaving Blue in the back of the van. Jack walked out of the farmhouse to meet him. He handed him a roll of notes.

"It's all there, Jack. Five hundred as we agreed. You can check it if you like." Jack took the bundle of notes and stuffed it into his jacket pocket.

"I trust you," he said. "Let's have a look at this bitch of yours, then." William opened the back door of the van and Blue jumped down onto the yard. Jack looked her over and nodded.

"Aye, she's not a bad one. She stands well and she's got a good head on her. She'll do alright for you. Bring her over to the barn and we'll see what Bruno makes of her."

The barn was some distance from the farm, well hidden in a copse of old trees. They could hear barking from the dogs as they approached and Jack yelled at them to shut up. He unlocked the padlock that held the heavy bolt in place and the door swung open. In the semi darkness of the barn William made out several dogs, all held by really heavy chains and most growling and barking ferociously as Jack went inside. He shouted at them again to be quiet. The one closest to Jack cowered for a moment and then growled at him and he struck out at the dog, catching it a blow with his fist. The dog bared its teeth and snarled at him.

"That one is due for a first fight soon. He's well ready for it too." Bruno was in the far corner, again tied with a heavy iron chain. Jack went to fetch the dog and put a thick leather harness round it before leading it out into the daylight.

Blue was very stressed at all of the barking and growling and lay down beside William, trembling.

"Get up, you stupid girl," shouted William, giving her a dig in her ribs with his boot. "We've got to get you with pups."

"You get her to stand still there and I'll let Bruno approach her. We'll soon see if she'd ready." Jack walked the dog towards Blue. He was powerfully built with massive shoulders and a huge neck. He lunged at Blue and, before Jack could hold him back, he snapped at her head and caught her left ear, tearing it badly. Blue yelped in pain and surprise. Jack decided to muzzle the dog and try again. This time Bruno mounted Blue and again the bitch yelped but the deed was done. Blue might be carrying Bruno's pups soon.

William was worried that Ben would ask questions about Blue's ripped ear and mopped at it with his handkerchief. It didn't look too bad, he thought. He put her back into the van and drove home. He reasoned that if he left her loose in the garden he could pretend that he didn't know anything about how she had done it.

Ben walked the short distance from the school bus to his house and was surprised to see Blue there waiting for him in the garden.

"Hiya, lass," he said, putting a hand down to pat her. His hand felt damp and when he looked more closely he saw blood on his fingers. Quickly he took her inside and called to his stepdad.

"Blue's hurt herself," he said. "She's got blood on her head." William came over to look at Blue, pretending to look concerned and surprised.

"She must have caught her ear on something outside," he said. "It doesn't look too bad."

"We should take her to the vet," said Ben. "It might need stitching."

"No, it'll be fine," said William. "Just clean it up and it will soon heal." Ben got some warm water and cotton wool and dabbed gently at Blue's injured ear. Blue winced a little, but she trusted Ben. The bleeding soon stopped and it didn't look quite as bad as Ben first thought.

He settled down at the kitchen table to make a start on his homework before his mum got home. Blue lay at his feet, glad to be back with Ben after her distressing outing to Jack's place. That night Ben decided to take her basket up to his bedroom and let her sleep there, a place where she was to sleep every night after that.

Chapter Six

Over the next few weeks Ben spent more and more time with Blue. He started to do odd jobs for the neighbours to make pocket money to pay for her food and took her for long walks to the park after school every day. He trusted her off the lead now and she never ran far from his side. She was great with other dogs too and they made a few friends on their walks. One, a big chocolate labrador dog called Harriet, belonged to a man who went jogging along the canal path. Harriet and Blue always greeted each other with a sniff and a friendly tail wag. Her owner was a member of the local kennel club and often stopped to chat with Ben. He really rated Blue; she was well put together, he said. She would do well in the local shows if it weren't for the split in her ear.

One afternoon as Ben was taking Blue on their usual trek beside the canal they ran into Harriet and her owner. Ben had learnt that he was called Alan. He stopped to say hello to Blue.

"I'm glad to have seen you today," he said. "We've got a fund-raising event coming up in a couple of weeks' time. It's a novelty dog show; not just for registered dogs but for pet ones too. I thought that you might like to come along with your staffie." Ben liked that idea. He had always thought that Blue was a super dog and it might be a fun day out.

"I'll put the details through your door next time I pass if you like," he told him. "Which house is yours?"

Ben told him that he lived at number six and the next morning, true to his word, Alan posted a leaflet through their door.

Novelty Dog Show to be held in the village hall and car park

Ben read through the leaflet with interest.

Classes for Best Rescue Dog, Best Crossbreed, Dog with Happiest Face....

There was quite a list. Blue's got a happy face, thought Ben. She might have the waggiest tail too. There was an entry fee of £2 a class and he thought that he could afford to enter at least one. Blue deserved to be shown off for the fine staffie that she was, he decided.

Soon it was Saturday and the day of the dog show. Ben was up early to brush Blue and to polish her collar and lead. She was looking good. Lucy had a day off work and the two of them decided to make a day of it. William was invited along too but wasn't interested. He'd sooner go to The Crown to have his usual pint with his mates there, he said.

Ben and Lucy walked to the village hall with Blue, her coat shining like fine velvet in the sunlight. They arrived to find the place full of cars and people with their pet dogs of all shapes, sizes and breeds. Alan and his labrador were there too and he waved to Ben across the car park.

"Good to see you here, Ben," he called as he made his way over to where they were standing. "Is this Mum?" He smiled at Lucy and held out his hand. "Ben's dog and mine are good pals," he told her. "We often pass one another on our walks."

Lucy smiled back. "Ben's very good at looking after his dog. I'm proud of him."

He asked if they had looked at the list of classes yet and decided which to enter. They hadn't, so Alan suggested that they tried the novice owner class and perhaps the one for the dog with the best coat.

Before long the entrants for the novice owner's class were called. Ben certainly wasn't the youngest competitor and he recognised one lad from his old junior school. They had to walk their dogs in a large circle and then ask them to sit. That was something that Blue had known already when Ben took her on and she did it well. The judge went around to each dog handler in turn, asking them questions about their dogs and how to care for them. When it came to Blue's turn she asked Ben to get her to stand and had a good look at her.

"You've a lovely girl there," she said. "When is she due to whelp?" Ben didn't know what that meant and told her so.

"It means to give birth to her pups," she told him.

"Blue isn't having pups," said Ben. "Maybe I've been feeding her a bit too much. She does look a bit

tubby." The lady judge felt Blue's tummy.

"She's certainly got pups in there," she said. Ben was shocked. He had no idea how that had happened. As far as he knew she hadn't been allowed out on her own to go near another dog. The judge agreed that Blue was a lovely animal but didn't give Ben an award in the novice owner's class. After the class was finished she came to talk to Ben and to Lucy.

"You have a wonderful dog there," she said "and you handled her beautifully. I couldn't give you a prize though because you hadn't known that she was in pup, and even a novice owner should know that." She wanted to make sure that they would be prepared to look after the bitch and the pups properly, and able to find good homes for them when they were old enough to leave their mother. She spent several minutes chatting to them both, giving them some good advice about puppy care.

She also suggested that Ben should enter the class for the dog that the judge should most like to take home because she said that she would love to own Blue. Ben decided to enter her in another class though, and at the end of the afternoon Blue had earned a second place in the class for the dog with the glossiest coat.

He asked his mum about Blue being pregnant as they walked home and she was as puzzled as Ben. She supposed that another dog might have got into their garden but had no real idea. It might be a bit of a problem if they weren't able to find homes for them. There was no way that they could keep both Blue and a litter of puppies for more than a couple of months.

William denied all knowledge of Blue's condition too for a few days but then he decided to tell Ben that he had taken her up to a mate's farm to show her off. His mate really loved dogs, he said, and staffies were his favourite breed. He made up some daft tale about how he had let Blue run around the farm fields one afternoon and how she had loved playing chase with his dog. Ben believed the story and asked about the friend's dog.

"Was it a staffie too, Dad? Where is the farm?"

"Too many questions, lad!" he said.

Ben decided that he would ask his friends at school to see if he could find homes for the puppies when the time came. Maybe one or two of the teachers might like dogs too. He thought that Blue would like to keep one and decided that two dogs would be company for each other when he was at school. He grew excited about the thought of having Blue's babies to look after and to play with.

Lucy nagged William a lot about him being irresponsible letting the bitch get with pups. Eventually he decided to admit that he'd been to Jack's place up at Firs Farm with Blue one day when he wanted to speak to him about another matter. He said that he had let her out for a run with his dog but hadn't known that she was in season. He said that he thought Blue was too old to get pregnant too.

William had become rather good at telling her lies over the years.

Blue changed shape over the next few days and one morning Ben's mum noticed that she was producing milk.

"I think that her pups are about to be born, Ben," she told him. "Get yourself off to catch the school bus and when you get home we'll sort things out for her." Lucy thought that the best place for Blue would be the old garden shed. It would have been lovely for her to have given birth to the pups in the kitchen but it was a small room and probably wouldn't be terribly safe. It tended to be a busy room too when they were all at home and when she was making food for her family.

When Ben got back from school they followed the lady judge's advice and went to prepare the shed so that it would be warm, clean and above all, quiet for Blue to concentrate on whelping. They spent a couple of hours moving the old lawn mower and garden tools out and scrubbing the floor well before putting down a layer of old newspapers to insulate it. They put down an old duvet and a couple of old blankets to make a bed for Blue too. The weather was warm and she and the litter of pups would be fine there for a few days.

Later that evening as Ben was finishing a rather boring piece of maths homework he noticed that Blue was pacing about his room, looking very restless. Then she went to the corner where he had thrown his school clothes and started scratching and pawing at them. Ben was always being reminded not to leave his clothes on the floor of his room but he still did.

"No, Blue! Don't do that, girl. I need those for school tomorrow." Ben called Blue and she followed him downstairs.

"I'm going to let Blue go to the shed," he told his mother. "She's about to have her pups, I think." He led her down the garden and opened the shed door. It was warm and cosy in there now and Blue went to the bed that they had prepared and started to paw at the blankets for a few moments before settling down. Ben really wanted to stay and watch to make sure that she was alright but had been told that he shouldn't as it would disturb her. He stayed with her for a few minutes and then told her to be a good girl and produce some super babies. He closed the shed and made his way back to the house to finish his homework.

Early the next day he got up, dressed and hurried to see Blue in the shed. He opened the door fully expecting to see her with six or seven pups but was so disappointed to see her lying in the corner where she had been the evening before, with a fat tummy still and no sign of any babies.

He let her out for a short run but soon she took herself back to her bed in the shed and went to lie down once again. He made sure that she had plenty of fresh water and food, although she didn't seem to be at all hungry, having hardly touched her supper from the night before. Ben really wished that it wasn't a school day as he wanted to be there for Blue and to see the pups being born, but he knew that he should leave her alone and not to fuss her too much.

Blue spent the next hours quietly on her bed in the shed, not quite sure what was happening to her. Instinct told her to sleep as much as she could but she kept wanting to change her position and felt very

restless. She went to her food bowl to nibble at a couple of biscuits but didn't really feel hungry after all. Eventually she pricked up her ears as she heard Ben's familiar footsteps on the path.

"Hello Blue," he said softly as he opened the door. "No babies yet?" Blue lifted herself off the blankets and walked over to greet Ben. She licked his hand as he bent down to give her a pat. He sat with her for a while until his mother appeared with some warm milk for Blue and mugs of hot chocolate for herself and Ben. The dog sniffed at the milk and then lapped at it with her long, pink tongue.

"She's enjoying that," said Lucy. Soon Blue returned to her bed and seemed to be panting slightly.

"We'd best leave her to it," she said to Ben."I can see that she doesn't really want to be watched now." They closed the door and went back to the house. Ben went down to check on Blue once more that evening before it was time for bed. He'd left the light on in the shed and opened the door and poked his head inside. Blue was lying on her side, panting still and this time she did not go to Ben. She seemed fine so he closed the door once again, leaving her to give birth to her babies.

The following morning it was Lucy who was up and about first. She made a mug of tea and took it up to her son.

"Ben," she called. "Have this drink and then you might want to get dressed and go down to see Blue and her little family." Ben sat up in bed and took the mug.

"So she's had them!" said Ben, excitedly.

"She has!" answered Lucy. "Four tiny pups, all looking well and all feeding well too." Soon Ben was up and dressed. It was Saturday so he had the whole weekend to look after Blue and her new family and could hardly wait to see them.

They were smaller than he has expected them to be, and had their eyes closed. Their faces looked wrinkled and a bit crumpled but they were very cute, he thought. They had the same blue black fur as their mum, although not much of it yet. They made little mewing noises, almost like kittens do, and snuggled against Blue as they suckled.

"You clever girl, Blue," he said gently. He put his hand out to feel her to make sure that she was warm enough. The tiny pups felt warm too and Blue was licking each one in turn as they fed. He wasn't quite sure why it happened but he found that a small tear was running down his cheek as he watched his little family. He would take the best care that he possibly could of them.

Chapter Seven

"Jack? Can you hear me? It's not a good line."

"That you, Will?"

He could just make out Jack's voice but it wasn't very clear.

"The bitch has had her pups," he said. "Lucy and the lad are going out this afternoon to do the weekend shop so, if you want to come round to have a look, there'll be no one about."

Jack agreed to meet William at The Crown and then they'd go to see the pups so that he could have his pick of the litter to complete their contract. A short time, and two pints, later William and Jack opened the shed door to where Blue was nursing her pups.

She was quite protective of her babies, naturally, but let William pick them up, one at a time to hand to Jack.

"They're healthy ones, sure enough, but there isn't a male dog amongst them," said Jack. "They're all ruddy lasses! Not a jot of good to me! They won't do for what I want at all!

"O come on, Jack! They're going to be fine when they've older and well grown. You'd be well able to

train one up and get some fight into it, surely."
William was fed up. He's paid very good money to
get the bitch in pup to Bruno and hoped to get a good
dog to keep for himself, as well as letting Jack have
the pick of the bunch.

"So how do things stand now?" William asked.
Jack looked thoughtful for a few moments.

"Tell you what I'll do," he said. "Your bitch is
doing a good job with those pups and she's obviously
a healthy one. Get her in pup again as soon as she
comes into season next and give me the male dogs. I
can't say fairer than that."

"So, a free return to your grand champion?"
William asked. "And if our Blue produces six male
dogs you'd want them all? Sorry but no way is that
fair!"

Jack considered the matter again. It was true that he
wouldn't want more than two pups really but it might
be many months before she gave birth again.
Eventually they made a deal. William wanted a large
male dog to raise as a fighter. Jack wanted one or
possibly two males at most. He didn't have much time
for smaller female dogs and William didn't really
want this litter of girls either. He'd give them a few
days with Blue and then take them away. Fewer
mouths to be fed and maybe Blue would come into
season sooner if she didn't have them to tend.

The two men left the proud mum and her little
family alone in the shed and walked back to the pub
where they remained for the rest of the afternoon and
most of the evening. They had been joined by a few

more of the Firs Farm Lads and, as the pints flowed, their tales of the best dogs and their wins became more and more embellished.

Back at the house Ben was helping his mum to unpack the groceries. She liked to shop at the local market on a Saturday as she could get some decent bargains there. She had got to know the traders and usually managed to pick up enough fresh fruit and vegetables for the week. Lucy went to the butcher's stall to buy half a dozen pork sausages for their supper that evening. Ben had asked if he had a bone that he might give to his dog too.

"I can probably find you something," he said. Ben told him about Blue's litter of pups and how she would need feeding up now. He found a ham shank that was a little too dry to sell and wrapped it for Ben. "Take this for her," he said as he put the bone into a carrier bag. "She'll enjoy that." He put a couple of kidneys in also. Blue was in for a treat that evening, thought Ben.

Supper that evening was to be toad in the hole again. Lucy was good at making decent meals cheaply which was just as well as her husband brought home very little money. Her wages from her cleaning job were just enough to cover the food and household bills and she had learnt to be careful with her spending.

Ben took the bone down to the shed and opened the door gently so as not to frighten the little family. Blue had eaten most of her food and drunk some of the water too.

"Here, Blue!" he said, holding the ham shank out to her. She sniffed at it and took it gently from his hand, carried it back to her bed and began to tear off the meat very neatly. She hadn't enjoyed freshly cooked meat for many months, only tinned dog food, and obviously loved it.

Over the next few days Ben watched as Blue took the best care of her little family, feeding them and licking them clean afterwards and letting them snuggle into her to keep warm. She was a wonderful mum. He decided not to give them names quite yet, partly because it was hard to tell them apart, but mostly because eventually their new owners would want to pick their own names for them. He had a fancy to keep the smallest one though and hoped that he would be allowed to have a second dog.

Over the next few days the pups grew on an almost daily basis. Ben told some of his school friends about them and one or two really wanted to adopt them. He didn't think that he would have any trouble in finding new owners for them but knew that they would not be ready to leave Blue until they were at least six weeks old.

Chapter eight

The following Wednesday there was to be another meet up at Firs Farm and William decided that the time had come for the pups to leave their mother and be of some use to him. That afternoon he found an old cardboard box and took it to the shed. He wanted to get them well away before Ben came home from school and Lucy from work. Blue was a trusting dog but was very anxious about her babies as William picked up each one in turn and bundled them into the box. She got up to follow him as he carried the box out of the shed and he shouted at her to get back and to lie down. He closed the shed door and carried the box to his van, started the engine and drove off.

Poor Blue was distraught, crying softly as she paced up and down searching for her missing pups. She sniffed at the blankets and pawed at them and sniffed all around the shed but they were nowhere to be found. Sad and bereft, she returned to the bed and lay down with her nose under her front paws.

Lucy was home earlier than usual that day and was already preparing supper when Ben returned home from school.

"Cup of hot chocolate, Ben?" she asked "or would you rather a cold drink?"

"Cold drink please, Mum," he said "but I'll just go

to see Blue first." Moments later he came running back to the house with Blue following close behind. His face was flushed and he looked very upset.

"Mum, the pups are gone!" he said. "They aren't in the shed; they're gone!" They both went out to look but the pups were not to be found. Blue searched every corner of the garden and went back to the shed twice but it seemed that they had gone.

As they walked back to the house Ben had a thought.

"I know what's happened," he said. Dad's taken them to show to the man who owns the male dog that Blue played with. "Don't worry, Blue!" he told her. "They'll all be home soon." Lucy smiled and really hoped that was what had happened but she had her doubts. She thought that they might have been stolen from the shed. There had been a few reports of dogs and cats going missing in the area and the pups were far too young to have been taken from their mother.

An hour passed and there was no sign of William or the pups. Ben was getting more and more worried.

"Do you know where Dad's friend lives?" he asked. Lucy thought for a few moments.

"It was somewhere called Firs Farm I think." she said. "If you find the telephone number we can telephone them to ask." She didn't really think that the pups would be there but it was worth a try. If William had taken them to show to his friend then it was time that they were brought back again. Ben picked up the telephone to call directory enquiries.

"What name please?" asked the voice. Ben explained that it was Firs Farm but that he didn't know the name of the people who lived there. He was told that they could find no entry for that address.

He was at a bit of a dead end, he thought. He had no idea where Firs Farm was and nor had Lucy. Ben went upstairs to attempt his homework but couldn't settle to do anything useful. Lucy called him down to have some supper later but he wasn't really hungry and just picked at it with his fork. That evening he went up to bed feeling as sad as he had ever felt. Blue's pups were missing and he had failed to protect them. Lucy heard him crying as she went upstairs to bed alone. There was no sign of William, and Lucy suspected that he had been down at The Crown yet again wasting time and money with his drinking friends.

It was well after midnight when the front door opened and William returned. He tried to walk up the stairs quietly so as not to wake Lucy but she was already awake and lying in the darkness. She reached out and switched on the bedside light.

"You're late, William!" she said. "I wish that you'd been home today because someone has been into the garden and taken Blue's puppies from the shed. If you had been here you might have seen them and been able to stop them. Poor Ben is terribly upset about it." William shrugged his shoulders and muttered something about it being a few less mouths to feed. He took off his jacket and Lucy noticed that his shirt was stained.

"William, whatever has happened?" Lucy asked,

looking alarmed. "That looks like blood. Have you hurt yourself?"

"No, it's nothing," he said. "I'm fine. It's not my blood." Lucy sat straight upright in bed.

"What the hell have you done, William?"

"Nothing that need concern you!" said William, crossly. "Now just forget what you've seen and don't ask me any more questions!" Lucy turned over and closed her eyes but all kinds of thoughts prevented her from sleeping. Had he been in a fight, she thought. Maybe he'd helped someone after an accident. She hoped that it had not been anything really bad. William had a temper. She knew that, but hoped him sensible enough not to have hurt anyone.

Chapter nine

Ben didn't manage to sleep well and was awake and dressed early the next morning. He wandered to the shed hoping against hope that whoever took Blue's babies would have returned them, but it was empty and lifeless.

"No sign of them then?" asked his mum, although she knew by the look on her son's face what his answer would be. Ben shook his head sadly. "Ah well, there's nothing that we can do now," she said. "Have some toast and I'll pack your lunch for school."

Ben still thought that his stepfather might have taken them to Firs Farm and was hatching a plan. Instead of catching the bus to school he would cycle there. He ate some toast and jam and had a mug of tea before setting off.

"See you, Mum!" he called as he left. It was a fine day and he quite enjoyed the ride to school. It took his mind off Blue's pups for a short while. He left his bike in the bike shed and made his way through the school doors and up the stairs to the library. He had a good ten minutes before registration and thought it would be enough time for what he wanted to do.

He opened one of the computers and entered his password. He wasn't quite sure of the website to use so simply entered the name of Firs Farm into the search box. It brought up a long list of entries and Ben started to scan down the page. One caught his eye; it was listed as being about six or seven miles from the school. He was able to find directions to get there after entering the postcode, and he printed out a map too and put the sheets of paper, carefully folded, into his coat pocket before heading off to his classroom.

After registration he picked up his bag and went back to the main hall and towards the doors. The school secretary saw him as he headed out of the school and asked him where he was going. He made up some excuse about going to check that he had locked his bike and she told him to hurry back so as not to miss lessons. He hoped that he wouldn't be seen as he cycled from the bike shed towards the school gates.

The route to Firs Farm looked an easy one. It was at the other side of the forestry land, a road that he had not been along before. He cycled down the road from the school towards the village, still hoping that he had not been seen. He didn't usually cycle to school but enjoyed going out and about with his friends during the holidays. He rode past the shops and the garage, past the housing estate and the church and out on to the road towards the forestry land. It was an uphill climb as he left the village and he was soon out of breath. He decided to dismount and to walk for a while. It was a warm day and he thought that he would have plenty of time to get to Firs Farm and back to school again before afternoon registration and, with any luck, no one would realise that he had missed the morning's lessons.

When he reached the forest he stopped to look at the directions again. He had to look for the first left turn that would take him through the woodland and out on the track towards the farm. It was further than he thought but if he found Blue's puppies there it would be worth any trouble that he might be in at school, or at home too if his stepdad got to hear about it.

The turn wasn't signposted and there was a padlocked gate at the entrance but he was able to lift his bike over it before climbing it himself and setting off on the next stage of the journey.

There were several side tracks but the main one was easy to follow. The track was rough and bore the imprints of tractor tyres but Ben rode steadily and before long he was nearing the other side of the forest. He stopped to read the directions once more, and to see how to find Firs Farm. He needed to find a ruined cottage and then a turn about a hundred yards beyond that. He rode on and soon saw the ruins of a small building that would once have been a woodman's cottage.

He cycled on and found the track shown on the map that he had printed. It looked quite clear of brambles and weeds and he thought that it must be in use regularly. He followed it for quite a way until he saw a house in the distance. That must be Firs Farm, he thought.

Soon he was at the lane that led up to the farm. Now that he was there he wasn't exactly sure of what to expect but he hoped that his stepdad's friend would tell him that Blue's pups were all there, warm and safe and well fed, and that he was going to bring them home that day.

The farm looked rather run down and Ben didn't see anyone about as he made his way to the door and rang the bell. He waited for a few moments and rang a second time but there was no reply. He decided to look round to see if the pups might be in one of the outbuildings and walked towards the shed.

The door was unlocked and he opened it slowly and called out to ask if there was anyone inside. Again there was no reply and so he went inside to see if there was any sign of Blue's babies.

The shed was almost empty apart from what looked to be an animal pen in the centre. There was a strange salty smell in the air and it wasn't nice. He walked to the pen and looked inside. It wasn't well lit but there was enough daylight flooding through the door to make out the horror of what he saw in that pen.

The walls were spattered with what he took to be dried blood and there was sawdust on the floor that held several pools of blood too. Ben thought that it could be a place where they slaughtered pigs or chickens but as he walked around the outside of the pen he realised that it wasn't so. Lying on its side was a large dog. It looked like a staffie, rather like Blue, and it was covered in bite marks and had a huge wound under its jaw and throat and a patch of ripped flesh on its hind leg. Ben felt as if he was going to be sick but put out a hand to touch the dog. It felt cold and solid and he knew that it was dead.

"What in the name of God are you doing here, you

nosey little idiot?" shouted a voice as Ben felt a hand on his arm. He spun round to see a large man, wearing scruffy and torn jeans and an old brown jumper, snarling at him.

Ben tried to speak but no words would come. The man grabbed him by both shoulders and shook him roughly.

"You tell me what you're up to!" he demanded. Ben managed to find a voice and mumbled that he thought that his lost puppies might be there.

"And what made you think that they might be?" asked the man. Ben started to explain that his bitch had a litter of pups and that he thought that his father had brought her to Firs Farm. His words came tumbling out and he wasn't making a lot of sense. The man asked who his father was and when Ben told him he looked surprised.

"Does he know that you're here then?" he asked. Ben explained that he didn't and would be cross if he knew that he had skived off school but he thought that he might have brought the pups to show to the man who owned the dog that had sired Blue's pups. The man thought for a moment.

"You want to know what happened you your little puppy dogs, do you?" he asked, in a mocking tone. His expression changed from the false grin to a wicked, sneering one.

"He did bring them here. He brought them to liven up the evening's entertainment. We threw each one into the ring one at a time and my Bruno ripped 'em to pieces. You should have heard 'em squealing as 'e crunched their 'eads off! It was great! You happy now, you little runt?"

Ben's face crumpled as he fought back tears.

"You killed them!" he screamed. "You're evil!"

"You're not wrong there!" he said as he pushed Ben to the ground. He gave the lad a hard kick in his ribs as he told him that he was to forget everything about what he had seen at the farm and not mention it to anyone. If he did, he told him, he would come after Ben and he would kill his dog and put him in hospital for a good long time and make sure that he was never able to walk or talk ever again. Ben struggled to his feet and he grabbed him again.

"Do I make myself clear?" he yelled right into Ben's face. Ben was terribly shaken and nodded and mumbled something.

"No get on your way back where you came from and don't ever let me see you round these parts again, you stupid little brat!" Ben limped towards the door and out of the barn, trembling. He picked up his bike and half walked, half ran with it towards the gate again to make his way back along the forestry track. He stopped at the old cottage and waited for a few moments to try to catch his breath and to gather his thoughts. His side was sore where he had been kicked and he was breathing in short, shallow breaths interrupted by sobs.

He knew that he should head back to the main road that led back to the village as quickly as possible. He wasn't sure if the man had been watching him as he left, or even if he might be following him. He was still feeling very shaken, and the sight of the poor dead dog was etched into his mind.

Eventually he reached the locked gate, managed to lift his bike over it, and soon was cycling back towards the village. When he got to the crossroads he had to decide whether to return to school or to make his way home. He would be back in good time for the lunch break and afternoon registration and perhaps he would not be in any more trouble that day. On the other hand if he went back home there was a good chance that his stepdad would be there and he would get a row for skipping school. He decided that school was the better option and cycled up the hill to the school gates, his side feeling very painful and bruised from the kick.

He managed to sneak back past the secretary and walked to the toilets to clean himself up as best he could. He rinsed his hands and face and combed his hair and straightened his clothes. It was almost time for the dinner bell so he hung around waiting for it to sound. When it did he made his way to the canteen to eat his sandwiches, hoping that none of the teachers had noticed his absence.

He answered as his name was called in registration later and went to the afternoon's lessons but his thoughts were not on his work and he was shouted at twice for not listening. Eventually the bell rang to mark the end of the school day and he made his way home, sadly. He had failed Blue and her pups were dead. They would have been cold, hungry and terrified too before they were thrown to his dog to be killed in such a horrible way.

He walked through the front door, dropped his school bag on the kitchen floor and ran to Blue. He put his arms round her and sobbed. "I'm sorry Blue," he said.

Chapter ten

Over the next few days and weeks Ben became more and more quiet and withdrawn. He had never been a top student but he had usually tried his best and completed homework on time. Now his work was going downhill badly and he was often late with assignments and projects, and constantly in trouble with his teachers for not working hard enough. His mother had noticed the change in her son but had put it down to his age and girl trouble. She decided not to embarrass him by asking him about it.

Blue thought less about her loss too and became a lively and loving dog once again, spending most of her time with Ben when he wasn't at school. Ben had told no one about what had happened at Firs Farm and how the pups had died but it played on his mind terribly. He had realised what was going on there and he was dreadfully upset to think of dog fighting taking place so close to home. He was even more appalled that his stepdad was taking a part in such vile things. He really wanted to tell his mum about what he had found at Firs Farm and about how his stepdad was involved but the thought of the wicked dog owner carrying out his threat was enough to prevent him from telling anyone. He knew that he would have to do all that he could to look after Blue and if that meant keeping it to himself, then he would.

It was a few weeks later when his group was asked

to choose a topic on which to give a talk for one of the English classes. Ben realised that he might be able to make something good come from the Firs Farm incident after all by deciding to use dog fighting as his subject. He reasoned that if more people were aware that it took place then something might help to bring to an end to it. He wrote a fairly detailed piece about it and, for once, put a lot of effort into his work. Some searching on internet provided lots of information on the topic and before long he was well prepared to give his presentation. He was actually hoping to make his fellow classmates aware of it and the awfulness of it.

The day came and the English lesson arrived where Ben was due to present his talk. He was to speak after one of his fellow pupils, Amie Peters, had given hers. Amie had chosen to talk about Stonehenge. She gave an interesting presentation about the origin of the stones and the superstitions surrounding them and used some pictures too. When she finished the class clapped and were invited to ask her any questions that they might have but nobody did.

Then it was Ben's turn and Miss Lowe called him up. He stood at the front of the class and read out the title.

The Evil Sport of Dog Fighting

The title came as a surprise to them and, as Ben began to speak about the so called sport, his classmates listened intently. He told them how the fights were planned and run, the cruelty involved in the training of the dogs and how bait dogs were used.

He told them that cats and other small animals were stolen to be thrown into the ring to encourage the starving dogs to kill them so that they would be fired up for fights, and how very large sums of money were placed on matches.

He spoke with feeling and a passion that surprised everyone in the room. At the end of his presentation the class applauded and was invited to ask him questions about it. One girl asked how he knew so much about it. He told her that he had researched it on the internet and she questioned him more about why he had an interest in it. He didn't know how to reply and had to stop himself from blurting out that it was what had happened to his pups. Instead he said that he had heard about it somewhere, probably on television. She was satisfied with his answers and said that she had been wondering if he was somehow involved in it. Ben told her firmly that he thought it the most cruel and evil of activities and had no right to even be called a sport. For once he had a very good mark for his work and Miss Lowe congratulated him on a most interesting and informative talk.

It was at that moment that Ben decided that he could keep what he had seen at Firs Farm to himself no longer and made up his mind to tell someone about it. He trusted his teacher and thought that she might be one of the best people to tell. At the end of the lesson he waited by Miss Lowe's desk and asked if he could have a word with her. She asked him to come back at break which he did.

He explained about Blue, her pups and his trek up to Firs Farm and what had happened there. He told her that his stepfather was involved and that he didn't know what he should do. Miss Lowe listened sympathetically but said that she was not really the right person to advise him on what he should do, if anything, and told him that he should speak to his parents about it. She said that some things happen in the big wide world that youngsters should not really have to be made aware of, and there were times when it was better to forget all about them and to carry on with their lives as if they had never happened. Ben had thought long and hard about it and wondered if he had been given good advice.

He couldn't even begin to think of telling his stepdad and thought that if his mother knew it would create so much disturbance in the family. On the other hand being told to keep it to himself and to forget about it didn't seem like good advice either. He had thought about telling his mother but was worried about the consequences if she knew. She would be sure to tell his stepdad and then both Ben and his mother would be in trouble. The matter needed more thought.

Chapter eleven

It was some weeks later that William took Blue back to Firs Farm to be put in pup again. Jack was still keen to get a male pup out of Blue, and his Bruno was a fine dog who threw good pups with plenty of spirit. He had managed to get her there and back without any trouble and Jack had kept his dog muzzled too after he had lunged at Blue the last time. In a few weeks she would give birth again and this time there should be some healthy male pups amongst them. William reasoned that if he let Blue nurse them until they were old enough to leave the bitch he could pass one or two on to Jack, say that he had found good homes for them, and Ben and Lucy would be none the wiser.

A couple of months later Ben began to notice the signs of Blue's pregnancy again but said nothing. She was putting on weight and he thought that he could feel movement inside her tummy too. He was worried that her pups would meet the sad end as the first litter and he made up his mind of what was to be done.

The following Saturday Ben took Blue out for her usual walk but, instead of walking to the park, he went to the police station, taking his dog inside with him.

"O dear!" said the desk sergeant. "Not another lost dog?"

"No way!" said Ben. "She's my dog but I need to talk to someone!" The officer asked Ben what it was about and he said that it was difficult to explain in a few words but that it was very important. The sergeant realised that Ben was a polite and nicely spoken boy and took his request seriously. Ben and Blue were invited into an interview room and asked to wait.

After a few minutes a woman police officer entered and asked Ben if he would tell her what it was all about. Ben had come this far and he decided to tell the whole story. He began from when they first went to see Blue after reading the advert in Free Ads. When he mentioned dog fighting she became far more interested. She listened carefully for a few moments, and then said that she wanted another police officer to hear his story too, and asked him if he would like a cup of tea or a glass of juice. He asked for tea with one sugar and then waited for that and for the police woman to return.

When she did she had another man with her. She introduced him to Ben as Inspector Morgan and said that he would like to hear what Ben had to say. It seemed that they were investigating a dog fighting gang in the area and that Ben's evidence could be very helpful indeed. Ben asked why they had not stopped the dog fights if they knew about them happening. Inspector Morgan explained that they had known about the activities at Firs Farm for some time but that the group was part of a far larger one and they needed to gather as much information as they could before making any arrests.

Ben felt so relieved to have been believed and not to have been told to go away and forget about it. When he had tried to tell Miss Lowe he felt that she was rather dismissive because he was a child, but these people were listening to him and taking him seriously. He was asked if his mother was involved in the dog fighting too and said that she most certainly was not and would be really upset if she knew that such things even went on.

It was suggested that he should tell his mother about the visit to the police station and that, if he liked, an officer in plain clothes would take him home and speak to her that day. His stepdad was to know nothing about it though. Ben was worried that his stepfather might be at home but reckoned that he would be at The Crown drinking with his mates.

It was decided that the woman police officer would give Ben and Blue a lift home and let them out in the next street. When Ben got back he would see if William was home or not. If not he would call the officer on a mobile phone that she had provided for the purpose. The plan worked well and, as Ben expected, his stepdad was at The Crown and would probably be there until supper time or later.

Ben explained that a lady wanted to have a chat with his mum and that she would tell her all about it. Lucy invited the officer inside and put the kettle on. After telling Lucy who she was she explained about how brave Ben had been in coming to the police station to tell his story. She said that they would like Ben to attend a safe house in the next town where he could make a full statement. Lucy was very shocked by it all! She knew that he husband was no saint but she found it very hard to believe that he was involved with a gang of dog fighters. The idea was just horrible.

It was arranged that they would go to the safe house on the following day and that William must know nothing about it. They were to carry on with their daily lives as usual. They knew full well that this would not be easy but it had to be done. At last Ben was able to tell his mother about his visit to Firs Farm and what he had seen there. She was upset that he had felt that he had to keep such a horrible experience to himself for so long, but Ben was pleased to be able to talk about it finally.

The next day they left the house, telling William that they were going to walk Blue along the canal and to the park. He wasn't terribly interested, preferring to watch Sunday television. They left him sitting watching a football match, a can of lager in his hand.

When they reached the park they were met by the plain clothed police officer who took them in an unmarked car to the safe house. It looked like every other house in the street and it was very comfortable inside with a kitchen and a sitting room that were far nicer than the ones in their own home.

They were offered tea and biscuits and afterwards Ben was asked if he understood why he had been invited there. He assured them that he did. Ben was taken into the interview room where he was told that they were going to record everything that he said. He was pleased to be helping and they spent quite a while talking about where Blue had come from and how the puppies had gone missing, about his trip to Firs Farm and what he had seen there. He told how he had been threatened by the man and how he had been far too frightened to tell anyone about it, fearing that he would carry out his threats if he knew.

Blue was in pup again and Ben said that he was very worried that the pups would go the same way when they were born. He was shown a series of photographs and asked if he could identify the man and was able to pick his face out easily from several that he was shown. They tried to reassure him that they would take every precaution to make sure that it didn't happen but nothing would stop him from being anxious about it.

The police would try to keep a watch on William's movements and asked Lucy and Ben to let them know straight away when Blue had given birth. When it was over they were given a ride home again and were dropped off in the road beside the canal. They were reminded again to do nothing at all that would give the game away, if such a thing could be called a game.

Ben and his mother were relieved to be told that the police had known about the Firs Farm Lads for some time and were waiting for the right moment to raid the place, but sorry that it was not going to happen straight away. They were concerned about Blue's pups but also that other dogs would be made to fight and to die before the raid took place.

Chapter twelve

Blue was growing larger and more restless as before and Ben and Lucy knew that she was about to give birth. This time though they decided to let her give birth in Ben's bedroom so that he could keep an eye on her. The school holiday was fast approaching and Ben wasn't going to let the little family out of his sight this time.

The following morning was the final day of term and Ben hoped that Blue would not produce her pups until he was there. Lucy was due a few days off too and she decided to take them then so that Ben would not be alone in the house if William did decide to take the pups this time.

Ben made an area in the corner of his room with old newspapers and a couple of old towels that his mum found for him , and Blue was happy to lie there awaiting the arrival of her new family. He could hardly wait for the school day to be over and the long holiday to come. At the end of the last lesson he returned to his classroom and packed his books, folders and pencil case ready for the break. He enjoyed school mostly, but this holiday was going to be an adventure and, he hoped, for all the right reasons.

William was in the kitchen when Ben walked in.

"Good day at school, lad?" he asked. Ben knew that

he had to chat to his stepdad as usual but inside he wanted to shout and scream at him for what he had done.

"Yes, it was ok, Dad," he said.

"That dog of yours has put on a bit of beef, you know. Are you giving her too much to eat?" William tried to pretend that he didn't know about Blue's mating but it wasn't so and Ben suspected as much.

"Dunno, Dad! Maybe!" said Ben. Blue was lying on Ben's bed when he went up to his room. She knew full well that she wasn't supposed to be there but gave Ben one of her "Please don't make me move!" looks and, just for once, she was allowed to stay. He sat beside her and gave her a reassuring hug.

"It's ok, Blue," he whispered. "This time no one will take your babies away." Blue had been restless again and Ben knew that he pups would be born very soon.

It was late that night, long after Ben had settled down for bed that Blue delivered her first pup. Ben was roused from his sleep by the same little mewing sounds that he had heard once before. He reached out to put the bedside light on and saw one little wriggly body lying beside Blue as she licked it lovingly, delighted to be a mum once again. A second pup appeared minutes afterwards and then a third, all wiggling and wriggling with life. Nothing must happen to these, thought Ben. Blue was doing a great job of birthing the pups so Ben turned over in his bed again and switched off the light, the sounds of their gentle cries comforting him and lulling him to sleep.

His mother came in with a mug of tea the following morning and smiled when she saw Blue with her new and very tiny babies, all suckling happily. Ben had been awake for a while and was watching them from his bed.

"Aren't they gorgeous, Ben!" said Lucy as she looked down at the little mass of legs and noses and paws. "We're going to need to keep a careful eye on Blue and her pups now."

"They're great!" said Ben. He sat up in his bed and took the mug from his mum. He held it with both hands as he watched Blue with her babies. "She's good with them isn't she?"

Lucy and Ben sat a while watching the little animals as they tried to crawl over the towels, their little pink tongues licking at everything as they got to know their new surroundings. After drinking his tea Ben climbed out of bed and went over to them. He lifted the small pups out, one at a time, to make sure that they were alright before placing them back with their mum.

"She's had four girls and two boys this time." He said. They were a lovely soft blue black colour, just like their mum, and Ben knew that he would need to keep a good watch on these. He didn't really want William to know about them but realised that it would be impossible to hide them for long.

He did not want them to have to live in the shed because it would not be easy to watch them day and night. It crossed Ben's mind to sleep there with them but he didn't really like the idea, although he would have done so. For the moment they were to live in his bedroom. Ben knew that he had to behave towards his stepdad as normally as he could and decided that it would be best to tell him about the pups. He planned to do so after he had eaten his breakfast if William was up and about.

William liked to have a lie in on weekends and he wasn't an early riser on weekdays either so it was mid-morning before he came downstairs, still in his pyjamas. Ben was back in his bedroom reading and keeping Blue company but Lucy was downstairs doing some baking for the weekend.

"Had you realised that Ben's dog was expecting pups again?" asked Lucy as she put some bread into the toaster and filled the kettle.

"No way!" William replied, trying to look and sound surprised.

"Yes, and this time we need to keep them safe." She told him. "Poor Ben was so distressed when the other pups disappeared."

"Someone must have been in to the garden shed and stolen those." William lied well.

Lucy told him that they would keep Blue and the pups inside the house now just in case it was to happen again. She knew full well what had happened to the other pups but could not say anything about it. She hated William for being involved in their deaths and couldn't bear to think of the foul and violent way in which they were killed. At least if they disappeared from the house there would be no one to blame other than her husband and he would realise that.

When they were a few weeks old it would be time to find homes for them and William thought that he could sell them to some of the lads in the Firs Farm gang for high prices, as well as giving one or two to Jack as payment for letting his champion sire them. If they turned out to be as strong and rough as Bruno they would be fine fighting machines, he thought. He had no thought for the poor dogs that were made to fight and were treated so very badly in their so-called training, being beaten, starved and forced to show as much aggression as they could.

Lucy didn't know what had turned her husband into such a monster but he most certainly had changed. He wasn't ever what she would have called a gentleman, like her first husband had been, but he wasn't a thug either. She realised at that moment that she had lost all love that she had for William and thought that it might be time for them to go their separate ways. For the present she had to stay there to keep an eye on Blue, the pups and William's movements. It wouldn't be a good time to leave and she really did not want to upset the police investigations either. Difficult as it was, she had to carry on her home life as normal. The time for decisions about the future would come later.

Chapter thirteen

The police force in the area had known about the activities at Firs Farm for some time and had been planning a major raid there. They had managed to get two of their officers to infiltrate the group although it had not been easy. It had taken them quite some time to win the confidence of Tom and William but Jim and his mate Miles had got drinking and chatting with them at The Crown and had eventually been invited to a meet at the farm.

They had been shocked at what they had witnessed but they had to go along with it and pretend to be part of the dog fighting set, placing bets and cheering on the winning dogs. They knew that their evidence would be vital to any arrests being made and dogs being saved eventually.

Jack held small meetings at the farm at least once and often twice a week for the local lads but they had a large meet planned there in a few weeks' time, the biggest of the season, and there would be dogmen and their animals from all over the North attending, some travelling very long distances to get there to pit their dogs against other champions. There were a good many arrests to be made and Operation Bloodhound had to be a success.

They had officers on standby prepared to go into action as soon as the word was given, with Inspector

Morgan leading the operation and hoped to close down several dog fighting circles once and for all.

In the meantime Ben and Lucy were keeping a very close watch on Blue and her family. Lucy had called Inspector Morgan as soon as they had been born and the police were doing their best to keep a watch on the movements of the Firs Farm Lads and on William in particular. They were still living in Ben's bedroom but were growing rapidly and were into everything, chewing his bedclothes and playing with his books and generally making quite a mess there. Ben knew that it would be time to find new homes for them soon and had been asking round at his school to see if any of his friends would be allowed to have puppies.

His mother thought that it would be best if they moved Blue to the kitchen so that she and the pups could go out into the garden more easily. They were almost four weeks old and too big to be living in the bedroom. Ben thought that it would be a good plan to make a run for them so that they would be safe outside on their patch of lawn.

He had seen a roll of chicken wire and some rusty iron posts in the next door neighbours' garden and he decided to ask if he could buy them, thinking that he might be able to use them to make a pen. He had some money saved from the odd jobs that he had been doing and hoped that they might not ask too high a price for them.

He went round to ask one morning while his mother kept guard on Blue and the babies. The neighbours were a lovely couple, in their early fifties, whose children had grown up and moved away. Ben knocked on their door and the wife answered, inviting him inside. Ben explained what he wanted and they kindly agreed that he could have the posts and chicken wire as a gift. They said that they had intended to get a few chickens but hadn't got round to it and the wire was lying in their garden doing nothing but cluttering up the place. They chatted together about Ben's dog and her litter of pups and thought that they would really like to own a dog again, now that they were semi-retired and had more time to take it for walks and to train it.

Ben wanted to keep at least one of the pups but had several homes to find for the others and thought that it would be good to have one living in the house next door. He invited them to come round to choose a pup if they did decide to adopt one. He thanked them again for the wire and posts and the husband helped him to carry them to his garden. It should be a simple thing to make a run for them and the posts were the sort that just pushed into the ground after being threaded through the wire, rather like giant sewing needles.

An hour later saw Blue with her six pups safely in their new pen, happily playing on the grass there.

"That's a grand run you've made there," called a voice from the next garden. "Can the wife and I come over to meet them all?" Moments later they were in Ben's garden chatting. They had been discussing things and had decided that they would love one of the pups; a girl if possible. They looked at them all and said that they couldn't decide between them and that they would be delighted with any one of them. They were like peas in a pod anyway, all miniatures of Blue.

At seven weeks or perhaps eight they would be big enough to leave their mum and go to their new homes so Ben and his mother had three weeks or so to watch them and to make sure that William did not take them away this time. One of the male dogs was becoming quite a mischievous character, always being the first to the food bowl and the liveliest of the pups. He was often gently told off by Blue when he tried to bite her ears or chase her tail. He was the one that Ben would most like to keep now. although he loved them all of course.

After an hours' run in the new pen they were looking really sleepy and Ben let them back into the kitchen, where they were to stay now. The outdoor run would be used when they were let out each morning but otherwise Ben wouldn't let them out of his sight until they left with their new owners.

The next weeks were quieter than his usual school holidays were. He didn't feel that he could spend much time going out and about with his friends as he would usually have done in a holiday because he really didn't want to leave the pups alone with his stepdad. He didn't trust him not to take them to Firs Farm as the first litter had been to be used as bait. The thought of them being killed was too much for him to contemplate. This time he had to make sure that they were safe.

Lucy had returned to her cleaning job but only for a few hours each morning now. She had explained to her boss that her son needed her at home more during the school holiday and he had accepted that. Money would be tighter because of the drop in her wages but they would manage somehow.

William spent his mornings in bed and was becoming even lazier than usual so he was often not up and around by the time Lucy returned from work. Between them they were able to keep a careful watch on the little animals.

Blue wasn't letting them feed as much as they did in their first couple of weeks and instead they were learning to feed themselves from the mash that Ben was giving them. Because he was so new to looking after pups he had borrowed a couple of books from the local library about puppy care and their weaning, and all seemed to be going well according to the advice that he had read. Soon it would be time to let them go to their new owners and he needed to make sure that they would go to good homes where they would have lots of company as well as the best of care.

Two of his school friends had been told that they could have dogs and the couple next door wanted one too. He wanted to keep the toughie of a male dog for himself so had just two more homes to find.

One morning as he was out in the garden watching Blue and the pups which were safely inside the pen he heard a voice calling to him. It was Alan, the man who had invited him to the dog show a few months before. He hadn't seen him for a while because he hadn't been walking Blue recently. He went to the gate expecting to see his dog too.

"Not got Harriet with you today?" Ben asked him. Alan explained, rather sadly, that he had lost his dog a few weeks ago. She had been getting old and had suddenly become unwell. The vet had diagnosed a tumour and it had seemed the kindest thing for her to be put to sleep when she began to suffer. He asked how Blue was and Ben invited him into the garden to see her and to meet the pups.

"Another litter?" asked Alan. "Your Blue was expecting pups at the dog show." Ben had to think quickly. "Blue did have a pup then but it wasn't healthy and it died soon after it was born, " he said. He hated telling lies but could not think of another way of explaining what had really happened to the first litter. Alan told Ben that he missed Harriet badly and had been thinking of getting a new dog. He would love to have one of Blue's pups if he could. Ben was delighted. He really couldn't think of a better owner than Alan.

"You wouldn't like to have two pups, would you?" Ben asked. He'd found homes for all of the others apart from the one that he wanted to keep. Alan told Ben that he would love to have two but that he thought one would be enough to train and care for. He said that he would like one of the girl pups and to put his name down for one. He asked Ben how much he was asking for them. Ben was surprised by this. He hadn't intended to ask for any money for them. Instead he thought it would be hard to find decent homes for them.

Alan explained that no one should give puppies away unless they were absolutely certain of where they were going. Too many were advertised as being free to good homes and often they ended up in very bad homes. Ben was so tempted to tell Alan that he knew something about where pups ended up when they were offered in adverts for nothing but realised that he could not tell anyone anything at all about the local dog fighters. It was to remain top secret.

Chapter fourteen

Saturday found William, Tom and a couple of the other lads having their usual pints in the pub and soon the conversation turned to the subject of the big meet. They talked at great length about the dogs that they might bet on, and if any other dog could beat Jack's dog, Bruno. Bruno had been put up against some of the best dogs in the area and had never lost a fight. William's money would be on him.

"So it's all set for next Thursday then?" asked Tom.

"Aye!" replied William. "Jack's getting everything ready and there'll be messages flying all over the North between now and then. This one's going to be big!" The men remained there talking until closing time. They kept their voices low when the Firs Farm meet was mentioned. They trusted no one outside of their gang.

The following day Inspector Morgan was joined in his office by Jim and Miles who had been drinking on The Crown the previous night. They were able to fill in almost all of the details about the meet; the day, the starting time and most of the organisers' names. It was time to get things moving. He called a meeting for the following morning and all available officers were to attend. Operation Bloodhound needed planning down to the last detail.

Meanwhile William was keen to complete the deal with Jack. Bruno's pups were worth good money at the moment but if his dog were to lose his next fight they would plummet in value. No one would really pay good money for pups that had been sired by a defeated animal.

The pups were about seven weeks old now and ready to go to their new homes. He'd call round at Jack's place in a day or two to take him the big male pup. He'd be satisfied to have just one William reasoned. It was a good strong sort and ready for a bit of hardening up now. His lad had made them all far too soft for his liking, always fussing over them and petting them. He'd keep one for himself too. Jack was happy enough for William to keep it up at Firs Farm. With luck it would become a fine fighter in time and would make him some decent money. He thought that he could sell the bitches on easily too. There was always a ready market for pups.

Inspector Morgan was very concerned about Blue's puppies. Ben and Lucy had done a great job of keeping them safe but the meet was coming up soon and if William was planning to take them there to throw into the ring as bait animals it might not be easy to prevent him. He decided to talk to Ben and to suggest that it was time to give them to their new owners now. Ben had kept him in the picture about his two friends from school, about Alan and the next door neighbours wanting pups and they had all been checked out to make sure that they had no connections with the Firs Farm Lads. He wanted to take one himself too. His wife was alone in the house for long hours and he thought that a dog would be good company for her as well as being a good guard. He'd ask Ben and Lucy if they would be happy with that.

He made a telephone call to the house to tell them what he had in mind. Lucy answered and he asked if she was able to talk. If William had answered the inspector would have pretended that he had dialled a wrong number, but all was well. He explained that it would not be easy to carry on protecting the pups now and that it would be wise to get them rehomed as soon as possible.

Ben knew that he would be sad to see the pups going to their new homes but realised that the time had come for them to be rehomed for their own safety.

William was in the pub yet again that afternoon so Ben was able to use the telephone without the risk of being overheard. He called his two school friends and Alan too, to ask them to come to choose their pups that day. Then he went to see the neighbours who were delighted to come round straight away to pick their new dog. They spent a few minutes playing with the pups and looking over each one before choosing the smallest of the girls. After making their choice the husband handed Ben a £20 note. He told him that they realised that he would have spent a lot of money on food for them and time on their care and thought it only fair, although Ben told them that they didn't have to give him anything. They had bought a new bed and food and water bowls already as well as some puppy food so they were all prepared. The wife cradled the little fur bundle in her arms as they took her to her new home just next door.

Before long Alan had called by too. He chose

another of the bitches and had brought a puppy sized collar and a lead to put on to his new pup. He'd even thought of a name for her by the time he left. She was to be called Saffie. Saffie the staffie! He insisted on paying Ben for his pup too and had come with five twenty pound notes in his wallet. He handed them to Ben and told him that he had to accept the money and that it was not open to discussion!

Later the same afternoon his school pals called with their families. They had been to the local pet shop for dog beds too and were both delighted to be puppy owners for the first time. They didn't offer Ben any money and he would not have accepted any if they had. He knew that they would need it for the pups to have their vaccinations and all of the other things that new dog owners have to spend on.

Blue was left with the two male pups now and seemed rather relieved in a way to have fewer little charges to feed and tend. Inspector Morgan called round after tea to make sure that all was well. He knew that William was still in The Crown drinking with his mates because, of course, he had insider information. Ben told him that he really wanted to keep the bigger of the male pups and offered the other one to the inspector. He said that his wife would be thrilled with the little animal and was really looking for forward to having a dog around the place again. He didn't stay long and, before he left, he told Ben and Lucy that the raid was to take place very soon and to do nothing out of the ordinary. They had managed well up to that point and must keep it up for a little longer.

Ben decided to let Blue and the last remaining pup sleep in his bedroom again that night and carried her bed up there rather than leaving them in the kitchen. He thought that she might be sad now that most of her family had left her and it was a wise decision. Blue took a little while settling but seemed to sense that it had been time for the other pups to leave and was happy just to curl up with her last pup and enjoy a good sleep without having to worry about feeding and washing so many babies.

The next morning William was up and about earlier than usual, before Lucy had returned from her morning's work. He went outside to the pen where Blue and the pups would be and was very surprised to see only one with its mum.

"What's happened to the other pups, Ben?" he asked, looking puzzled. Ben explained that he had been asking around his friends for a few weeks to find new homes for them and that they had all gone to their new owners the day before apart from the one that he wanted to keep. William looked cross when he heard this.

"Whatever did you do that for, you twit?" he asked. "They were good dogs. We could have sold them."

"I wanted to be sure that they were going to nice people," said Ben. "They've all gone to people whom I know, so I'm sure they'll be looked after." He didn't mention that he had been paid for two of them. He wanted to keep that money for Blue's keep and for the pup too.

William told him that he knew several friends of

his who would have given them good homes too, and would have paid decent money for them. Ben said that good homes were far more important than money. William thought for a moment. He needed a male dog to complete the deal with Jack and there was only one pup left.

"We can't really let you keep two dogs, Ben," he said. "This house is too small and if they ever need the vet we would struggle to afford it. Remember why Blue's owner gave her away? It was because she was costing too much to keep." Ben knew that it wasn't the exact reason but didn't argue.

"One of my mates really wants a puppy," said William. "He promised one to his son for his birthday." He picked up the pup from the pen and looked at it. He saw that it was a male and said that it would do well.

Ben really didn't want him to take the dog but didn't know how to refuse him. He had little choice, he thought.

"Will his son be nice to him?" Ben asked.

"O yes. He's a good lad. He'll take care of it." William put the pup back in the pen with Blue and went back into the house to make a telephone call. Ben waited for a few seconds and then crept up to the door to listen when he heard him lifting the telephone off the wall bracket.

"I've got your pup for you, Jack," he said. "Shall I bring it over or would you like to come round for it? It's a good strong male dog just as we agreed."

William spoke for a few moments more but Ben didn't stay to hear the rest of the conversation. Perhaps his stepdad really did have a friend with a son who wanted a staffie pup for his birthday. He hoped so. He went back to play with Blue and the pup. He had really wanted to keep it but realised that he couldn't argue about it.

William came out to the garden to talk to him again. He said that his friend was coming round in a short while and that he would take the last pup for his son. Ben felt very sad to be losing it as it was the one that he wanted to keep. He decided to stay and play with the pup until it was collected. Then he would have Blue all to himself again and could start to take her out for longer walks once more and would try to forget all about the pups, the forthcoming raid and the dog fighters.

Before long a van drew up outside and a man got out. He called to William who was waiting by the gate. Ben's heart almost missed a beat. Immediately he recognised him as the man from Firs Farm who had shouted at him and terrified him all those weeks ago. Now he had come for Blue's puppy and Ben feared that it would end up being killed in the same horrid way that her first litter had been. He wanted to shout and scream at the man and at his stepfather too that he wouldn't give the pup away but he knew what he had to do. If he said anything now it might jeopardise the whole police operation and Ben knew that.

"What do you think of this one?" asked William as he bent to pick up the pup. He held it out to the man who took it by the scruff of its neck.

"You did well with this one," he said, looking over the pup carefully. "I'll take him!" Ben walked over to them both.

"I hope that your son likes the pup," he said, pretending that he didn't recognise the man. "My stepdad said that it is a birthday present for him." The man looked a little taken aback, first by the story about a son and a birthday present and also because William's lad had not appeared to recognise him.

"If he doesn't like him you can always bring him back," said Ben. "I sort of wanted to keep one puppy."

Jack shook his head at Ben and thanked William and muttered something about seeing him soon, walked with the young dog to his car, opened the boot, put it inside, and then got into the driver's seat and drove off.

William went back to the house, pleased to have completed the deal, but rather fed up that he hadn't got a dog of his own from Blue. Ben stayed outside with Blue waiting for his mum to come home from work. He slipped on Blue's lead and set out to walk along to meet her. They met up as Lucy was coming around the park road and Ben told her what had happened. He said that William had given the last puppy away to a friend of his but didn't say that it had gone to the man from Firs Farm. He realised that his mother would find it very hard to keep that to herself and thought it best to say nothing.

The house seemed rather empty without the little family of pups. They had become used to hearing their little cries and their gentle snuffling when they were asleep and Ben and his mother missed that. Blue seemed sad now that her last pup was gone. Ben really hoped that nothing bad would happen to it before the meet and the police raid but now it was something of a waiting game.

If he could have he would have made his way to Firs Farm again to rescue the pup, but feared what would happen if he were to be caught. He really couldn't risk it a second time.

Chapter fifteen

It was the day of the meet and Inspector Morgan had called a final conference to ensure that Operation Bloodhound would run to plan. He had the two officers, Jim and Miles, in the Firs Farm Lads group and a further one in a large group that was travelling from further north. They had unmarked cars along the routes to Firs Farm and officers ready to block the both exits to the barn where the fight would be held and to the farm drive and tracks. There would be RSPCA officials there too, to rescue the dogs and a vet on hand to help with any injured animals. It was to be a big operation and had to be successful.

William and Tom wanted to be at the farm in time to get a good seat and to place bets before the odds were raised sky high. Jack had managed to lay on several barrels of homebrew and they were offered pints as soon as they arrived. They could hear the dogs barking in the sheds and the atmosphere was electric as the barn began to fill with people.

Many had travelled for well over a hundred miles to get to Firs Farm and now waited in anticipation for the first fight to begin. There were 4 x 4s and old vans parked all along the farm track as well as in the yard and caged dogs being unloaded. There were some kittens and a couple of cats in a basket too but so far no sign of Blue's pup although it wasn't easy to see exactly what was happening with the crowds that were gathering.

Betting was keen and a couple of youngsters were to fight first. The officers knew that they could not stop the event before a fight had taken place because they would have no evidence to produce in court if they hadn't witnessed a crime. Jim had managed to find a position close to the pit and Miles, the other officer, stayed close to the entrance, chatting to Jack. Soon it was time for the first roll.

Two dogs were brought into the pit by their handlers and the referee told them to keep their animals behind the scratch line until they were told to start. The dogs were both young and about to face their first fights in the pit, although they would have been trained to attack bait animals well before that.

The handlers were told to face their dogs and both turned their animals towards the centre of the pit so that they could see each other. One dog, Logan, was snarling and eager for action but the second dog was obviously terrified.

"Release your dogs!" shouted the referee and both handlers did so before leaving the pit. Logan lunged towards the other dog, his owner shouting at him to fight. The second dog didn't turn away but opened his jaws to attack.

"Fight, you stupid dog!" his handler yelled at Jupiter. "Get him!" Logan was faster though and got him by the neck. He sank his teeth into Jupiter's flesh and the dog yelped in pain, struggling to get free. It managed to get a hold on Logan's front leg and bit hard. Jupiter had strong jaws and managed to tear a large piece of skin and flesh from it.

The floor of the pit was beginning to get spattered with blood as the dogs fought and the two infiltrators were ready to signal for the police officers to open the doors and put an end the activities.

The two dogs fought on, growling and snarling, each trying to get a hold on their opponent. Eventually Logan lunged towards Jupiter in a final effort to end it all and his fangs bit into the other dog's side, ripping through the muscle wall and making a massive tear. Jupiter knew that he should fight on or fear being beaten by his handler but couldn't. His pain was too great and he had no fight left to defend himself.

"Get up, you bloody thing!" His handler was yelling at the top of his voice now but to no avail.

At that moment the barn door was flung open and a voice shouted "POLICE! Stay where you are! We've got the place surrounded and the other exits blocked." The crowd fell silent. All that could be heard were Jupiter's cries as he lay bleeding in the sawdust on the pit floor.

"We need the vet in the ring please now," called Jim, still standing beside the ring. One of the men standing close by pulled a knife from his pocket.

"You bastard!" he growled. "You bloody, double-crossing bastard! You betrayed us!" Jim grabbed his wrist.

"Drop the knife now, or you'll be on a charge of attempted murder as well!" He dropped the weapon, still seething with anger as the vet made his way to the pit and to where the injured dog lay. He could see that Jupiter was dying and put out a hand to rest on the dog's shoulder.

"It's ok now, old chap," he whispered as he felt the dog's front leg looking for a vein. "You didn't ask to be made to fight, did you?" Gently he slipped the needle in and pressed the plunger. "No one will make you fight again," he said as he stroked Jupiter's head. Jupiter closed his eyes, the pain leaving his body as he fell into the deepest of sleeps, finally sensing the sound of a kind voice and a gentle touch in his last moments.

The arresting officers were kept very busy for several hours that evening. They had police vans working in convoy ferrying those taking part to the station where they were formally charged before being released on bail, and Jack was taken into custody and would remain in a police cell for the night.

Lucy and Ben received a call from Inspector Morgan later to tell them that the raid had been successful and to thank them both for their help. He suggested that they should say nothing about their involvement when William returned home. He had been one of those arrested, of course. Ben asked about his puppy and was dismayed to be told that it hadn't been found but that there were animal welfare officers still searching the outbuildings and that they would hear if Blue's pup was found. He thanked them both again for their help before ringing off.

Ben decided to go to bed, rather than wait up to see his stepdad, and took Blue up with him. That night he let her curl up and sleep on his bed. Eventually he fell asleep but slept fitfully, his head too full of thoughts of Firs Farm, Blue's puppies and his stepfather being involved in such activities.

It was close to midnight when Lucy heard William turning his key in the lock.

"Not gone to bed yet, love?" he asked. He looked ashen-faced as he went to fill the kettle. "Cuppa?"

Lucy declined the offer of tea and decided to ask him where he'd been so late on a Thursday evening. Saturday was usually his late night, she told him. William said that she would find out soon enough that he had been charged and thought it might be better to come clean about it all.

They stayed up talking late into the night. William explained that he had been involved with the Firs Farm gang but that he had done it just for the money so that he could provide for Ben and for her. Lucy listened but didn't believe a single word of it. She knew what had happened to Blue's first litter of pups and to the last one of her second litter too, the little male dog that Ben had so wanted to keep. William had given it away to the gang leader. How could she carry on living with him after that?

"William," she said sadly. "I hate what you've done and what you've become. We can't go on like this. It's a sham of a marriage now." William put his head in his hands. He didn't want to lose Lucy or Ben either but the situation was entirely of his own making and he knew it.

"So what happens now?" he asked. Lucy shook her head. She couldn't carry on living with William and the house was still in his name so he would be unlikely to want to leave his home. William decided to sleep on the sofa for what was left of the night.

Chapter sixteen

Lucy was awake very early the next morning. She went into Ben's room to talk to him and found him fast asleep with his arms round Blue who was resting beside him, her head on the pillow.

"Ben," she called. "Are you awake?" Ben stirred and Blue raised her head from the pillow. "Ben, how would you feel about moving away from here?" Lucy asked.

"You probably guessed that William was one of the ones who got arrested last night." Ben said that he had. His mother went on to explain that she had decided that she could no longer live with William after what she knew about him now.

George, her first husband, had a sister who lived in Wales. She had the family farmhouse, inherited after her parents died and she had always said that there would be a home for Lucy and Ben if ever they needed one. Lucy would ring her that morning to see if the offer was still open. They had visited her there a couple of times and Ben liked the house and the area very much, and he was fond of his Aunt Beth too. He could understand why they couldn't live with William now. He didn't trust him around Blue either.

Lucy made the call to Beth later that morning. William had got himself up and about earlier and had gone out, she knew not where, and was beyond caring too. All she wanted to do now was to get away, and get herself and Ben to safety, with Blue of course. She explained something of what had happened, and

Beth said that they were to pack a few things and that she would drive over to collect them as soon as she could later that afternoon.

It didn't give them long to pack clothes and valuables into whatever cases and bags they could find. Beth had promised to bring her land rover to collect them as it could carry more luggage than the little run-around car that she used for shopping trips. After a few hours they had lined up lots of black bin bags beside the door as well as their suitcases and Blue's bed and feed bowls.

Ben had given up all hope of seeing the last puppy again and was upset about that but he was relieved to be moving away. He knew that the Firs Farm Lads would be out for revenge and they would soon realise that William's wife and stepson had been involved.

Lucy thought it sensible to phone Inspector Morgan to tell him their new address. He said that he thought it would be a wise move to get out of the area. The members of the Firs Farm Lads gang were a rough lot and they would be safer well away, at least for the time being. William had been released on bail but would be making a court appearance soon and would probably receive a fine as well as a ban on keeping any animals for many years.

Lucy asked again if they had managed to find Ben's puppy and was told that the RSPCA and the animal welfare officers had taken a number of dogs away from Firs Farm and that he would make some enquiries but not to expect too much as if might have been used as a bait dog.

Beth arrived later and they all helped to load the cases and bags into the back of the land rover. They had left a lot of their belongings in the house but thought that they might return for those sometime. Now they just wanted to get away from the bad memories and the stress of it all. Lucy climbed into the front seat and Ben and Blue settled in the back, surrounded by carrier bags, and settled down for the long drive to Wales. It was a good four hour drive and soon Ben found himself drifting off to sleep, resting his hand on Blue's soft fur.

Back at the animal shelter there were more dogs arriving from the Firs Farm raid. Some were in a very poor state, being thin and undernourished, and others had marks and scars from untended wounds acquired both in and out of the ring. The vet had been called in again to destroy a few of the dogs that were in such a bad condition that they could not be treated or made well. The RSPCA officers had found a small staffie pup too in a shed fastened with a heavy chain and large leather collar. It was very cold and not more than a few weeks old, they said. It would be an easy one to rehome. Puppies were far easier to find new homes for than older dogs, particularly those with health and behavioural problems as the ones rescued from the raid would have.

Eventually Lucy, Ben and Blue arrived at Beth's home in Wales. They decided to leave most of the bags in the vehicle until the next day and just to take the suitcases inside so that they would have their nightwear, tooth brushes, etc.

Beth had left a casserole in the slow cooker and had

prepared some mashed carrots and swede too and soon they were all settling down to a hot meal in the old farmhouse kitchen. The aga was warming the place and Blue had made herself very much at home on the rug in front of it.

They began to fill Beth in on the details of the past few weeks and months and she was very shocked to hear about it, and how William had turned out. She remembered him as being a bit of a rough diamond but no worse than that and certainly not a criminal. How people can change, she thought.

For the first time in several weeks Ben and Lucy were able to sleep peacefully, and Blue enjoyed a cosy night too, sleeping beside the aga. Lucy had not left a note for William to say where they had gone and hoped that he wouldn't guess or try to contact her or Ben again. He had said that he wanted nothing more to do with his stepfather now.

The following morning they were again sitting round the table in the kitchen enjoying boiled eggs collected that day from the hen house and homemade bread, when the telephone rang. Beth answered and called Lucy to the phone.

"Hello again," said a voice. "Inspector Morgan with some good news for you, I think." He told her that the animal shelter and replied to his query about Ben's puppy and had found a small black Staffie pup there of around the right age. They were very keen to return it to Blue and to Ben and wondered if it would be alright if one of the volunteers from Staffie Rescue could drive it there to deliver it that day. Lucy replied that it would be great and thanked him very much.

She decided not to tell Ben though, thinking that it would be a lovely surprise for the boy after all the upset of recent weeks, and there was a chance that it wasn't his puppy too, of course.

Ben decided to go for a wander round the fields with Blue after breakfast. It was a sunny day and he loved the freedom of the place. Ben thought that he would be very happy living here. The mountains looked stunning as he made his way down to the stream that ran through the lower pasture. Ben tried to get Blue to go in for a swim but she wasn't used to water and refused.

The two made their way back to the house where Beth had the kettle on ready to make hot drinks for them all. She enjoyed having a family to look after again. Her own daughter was much older and had left home years ago, and her husband had died a couple of years ago and to tell the truth she was very glad of the company now. She hoped that Lucy and Ben might decide to make their home there. They spent the rest of the morning unpacking bags.

They had managed to bring most of their clothes as well as books and some of Lucy's favourite ornaments and trinkets. It took a while unpacking it all but eventually it was done. They had packed the washing too and Lucy had put two large loads through the machine and hung them outside on the line to dry in the sunshine. Ben was helping her to hang out the final load when a car pulled up on the yard.

The driver got out and asked if he was at Ty Gwyn Farm. Ben told him that he was. He explained that he was called Linus Clerk and that he was a volunteer driver for Staffie Rescue. He'd been contacted by the animal rescue centre near to their old home. He went to the back of his car and opened it to reveal a large crate. He unfastened the top door of it and gently lifted out a small furry bundle and held it out to Ben.

"Does this little fellow look familiar?" he asked. Ben's face broke into a huge smile as he held out his hands to take the puppy.

"That's Blue's pup!" he said. "I never thought to see him again. I thought he'd been killed." He cuddled the pup close to him and Lucy invited the man inside for a cup of coffee.

"I wanted to keep this one," said Ben. "My stepdad gave him away though and I really thought that I wouldn't see him again."

"Well," said Lucy. "You're going to have to think of a name for him now, and you'd better ask your Aunt Beth if you are allowed to keep two dogs here too."

"Well, we can't see a little chap like him going back to the shelter can we!" said Beth. She'd come out to see who had arrived when she had heard the car on the yard. She loved dogs and was as delighted as Ben to have the puppy there.

Blue got up from her bed when they walked into the kitchen. As soon as she saw her pup her tail began to wag furiously and she ran to Ben who was still holding it in his arms.

"So, what are you going to call the little fellow then?" asked Mr. Clerk. Ben thought quickly.

"Well," he said. "I think that he should be named after you." He put the little animal down and Blue nuzzled him before licking him very gently with her long tongue.

"There, Linus," he said. "Back safe with your mum! No one is ever going to try to hurt you again," he whispered.

. 28018406R10057

Made in the USA
Charleston, SC
29 March 2014